the unsung letters

BY GEORGE THOMAS

BlueRoseONE.com
Stories Matter
NewDelhi • London

BLUEROSE PUBLISHERS
India | U.K.

BlueRose ONE.com
Stories Matter
NewDelhi • London

For permissions requests or inquiries regarding this publication, please contact:

BLUEROSE PUBLISHERS
www.BlueRoseONE.com
info@bluerosepublishers.com
+91 8882 898 898
+4407342408967

ISBN: 978-93-7139-134-4

Cover design: Daksh
Typesetting: Tanya Raj Upadhyay

First Edition: July 2025

Preface.

The Unsung Letters is a journey into the quiet corners of the heart–

those places where words often hesitate, where emotions linger in silence, and where feelings remain unspoken. This collection of poetry is not just a gathering of verses, but a series of emotional echoes–letters never sent, thoughts never voiced, and love never confessed.

Each poem in this book is a fragment of a story, a whisper of a moment, an attempt to give voice to what we often leave unsaid. They speak of longing and healing, of vulnerability and resilience, of the tender and the torn. Through these verses, I invite you to listen closely–to the hush between words, to the depth beneath a sigh, to the music of the unsung.

Whether you find yourself in these poems or simply pass through them, I hope they offer comfort, clarity, or a spark of connection. May you feel seen, understood, and perhaps, just a little less alone.

With all the unsent love,

George Thomas xo

Table of Contents

Rebirth.

So, this is farewell to the ways of old,
We've come so far from where we once stood,
But every end sparks a tale anew,
Last night's shadows are now lost in the morning's hue.

Reborn, yet the scars still softly remain,
In peace, I bask, no need to explain.
What stirs within this quiet flame?
Is it the truth, or simply me reclaiming my name?

The breeze now sings a gentler song,
Mystic, wild, where hearts belong.
No longer chained by wrath or fear,
I'm found, not lost, forever near.

The air breathes hope, fresh and bright,
A day more vivid than any night.
No phantoms whisper, no voices call,
At last, I feel one with it all.

In harmony, we rise as one,
Beneath the moon, beneath the sun.
Held by love without an end,
Above, with you, where spirits ascend.

Velvet sin.

The time is now to let go, calm and composed.
The one I loved is long since gone,
Now I embrace all that flaws,
A thousand faces, names unknown…

Yet I feel confined in that lie…
Each fleeting touch, each passing eye,
All the same, a perfect stranger
Whispering yet another goodbye.
And in between love blurs complacency.

Money sway the carnal,
Sins crave the burning desires…
She makes it rain on the pole,
While I drown myself in her skin.

There is nothing else I could go than to waste my life like a fool,
Bend for me one more time like a good girl!
Am I cruel? Or just in need?
Can you try me as I please…

Love scorches like a fevered flame,
So, let's just cool off with our clothes off!
Let our cold heartbeats dance our bodies,
And succumb to the sweetness of sinful pleasures.

Two graves apart.

I dreamed alone for far too long,
Even with you near, something felt wrong.
Your touch was there, but not your flame,
Your heart, a frost that knew no name.

I found you drowning in the shallow tide,
Held you close, with nowhere to hide.
Never cared what the world uttered,
Except for what your eyes said.

Beloved in the path of the sin,
I drew your soul to dance within!
To ignite that spark you always had within to give in that silent will,
To let your morals drown by the kiss of dawn.

Carnal pleasures were our only connection,
The undying lust kept us coming back in each other's arms,
The fire between your thighs and the warmth between your bosom,
Shattered the shackles that kept me.

You know my truth was always you,
But yours, a lie I still cling to.
A past we lived and loved, suffered and prospered.
To end up like this, two graves apart in dirt.

Crimson tea.

Smooth as satin, wild as flame,
With fire and blood, she staked her claim.
The grace of saints upon her brow,
She walked the path of purpose, somehow.

Grief carved wisdom in her bones,
In a world of choices, harsh and lone.
With hunger fierce, she dared to stake
Her claim, a slice of life's sweet cake.

When time grew dark and hearts turned stone,
And those she loved left her alone,
She gazed at skies so vast, so blue,
And wondered why the pain below felt true.

In the dance of love and spite,
She strung her soul to echo right,
A melody, half growl, half grace,
That made the proud ones pale their face.

Still, she walks that narrow trail,
Where endings come, and mortals fail.
But to arrive, she gave her fire,
A sacrifice none else desire.

And now, what stirs within her chest?
A longing deep, a thirst for rest.
To lay her burdens, breathe, be free,
And sip once more that crimson tea.

Global aura.

I inhale that hydroponic flame,
Exhale peace, good vibes in my lane.
Raise a glass to the life I chose,
Grateful every time my aura glows.

Proud, I found my stride,
Ten toes grounded; spirit wide.
Legends posted on the stoop,
Gold chains, bricks, old-school roots.

Money moves how I pursue,
No more broke, no more confused.
Grind so hard my pulse gets paid,
Every heartbeat makes a way.

She spins on poles, rain starts to pour,
Wild on the sheets, she wants encore.
Future queen, I see your shine,
Let's dine, smoke a cloud and make love divine.

Is this your norm? the devil pried!
From pole to pole, worldwide! I replied.
None do it like me and my crew,
No one can touch what we do.

Rhythm’s frame.

Love her enough to let her go,
From dusk till dawn, I dwell in the symphony of her touch…
At mornings breeze, I say goodbye,
Then drift toward blooms with nectar I must try.

Easing pain with fleeting highs,
Numb to feel, yet I feel her cry!
Whispers of comfort between her arms,
I lay, letting go of what I am.

But now, I feel the rain, the sunlit rays,
The butterflies that dance in dawn’s first blaze.
The sky, a canvas brushed in hues divine,
A rainbow arcs, the path ahead aligned.

Above the clouds, I float with clearer mind,
Stronger with each test I’ve left behind.
Fortune smiles, on one's fortunate to see,
As the wheel of fate turns endlessly.

Seasons change, but the weather is pleasant.
The moment greets me, one of a rare find.
The world has changed, yet here I stand, the same,
A different song within the rhythm’s frame.

Whispers of Comfort.

Butterflies hum with joy in golden rays,
While the sun spreads hope in endless ways…
You remind me of the love the world beacons,
Everyday has a happy ending.

Is this what mother's warmth is called?
Belly full and hands warm,
The serenity and safeness,
The love no words could embrace.

Rain drops awaken the scent of the earth,
Lilies and the roses smile...
Where lush greens cover the fields like wild weeds,
A fleeting high the heart enslaves.

Just as seasons manipulate one's emotions,
Life is a notion, a ride with ups and downs,
The fear you feel is just the thread,
That weaves the path where freedom will grow.

Like ripples dancing on a stream,
What seems to be blurred may soon become clear,
Trust what's etched in the heavens for you,
A simple truth, a humble belief that God is pure.

Moonlight rhythm.

Like a girl dancing in the flames with diamonds raining…
She sways the crowd's hearts away with awe…
Making you wish a minute more in your life,
To see her more, to feel her rhythm.

Making you feel love, mind and soul alike…
A breath you wished you had heard more closer,
A heartbeat you know you want in top of yours,
A feeling you know but know it's not over yet.

So, kiss me now, I need those hands around,
Dance with me, push those hips close…
Touch me till you feel me,
Hate me till you want me more.

Cradled gently, safe and warm,
In this hush forever, come what may…
Then hum a lullaby, soft and low,
To let this perfect moment glow.

And when your heart knows it could stay,
Let your feet run to her and hold close…
And dance with her under the moonlights gleam,
Sweeter than any midnight dreams.

In the Wake of Her Love.

There she stood, a beacon bright,
Reviving my soul with golden light.
A spark rekindled, once thought lost,
Her smile, a joy my heart embossed.

Her beauty shadows rainbows,
Of painted skies and morning dews.
Her breath, a fire igniting my chest,
Her words, my hope, my soul's request.

Her touch, her kiss, like embers warm,
Our bodies meet a perfect storm.
Desire burns in passion's flight,
A lust, so pure like the nightingale's song.

The past burdens that blistered once,
Hence to fade away with your soothe!
The surreal sensation you hypnotize,
Got me feeling blissful with you beside.

The taste of her is what my tongue lingers…
For in her I find solace…
For in her arms, I've found my heart enslaved,
And yearn to love-again, complete.

Midnight kisses.

From the moment I saw you,
The world gleamed in a different light.
You chased away my shadows,
And wrapped me in your heaven-kissed wings.

Lost in your gaze, I am spellbound,
The scent of your skin better than the morning lily dews,
I find myself found within you…
And when I'm within you, we become one.

A world of bliss within your kiss,
I crave your touch, your every taste.
Untamed desire, a fiery embrace,
Cleansing our souls in passion's mist.

You took care of me when I stood low,
Your heart, a thousand flowers bloomed.
Your joy–you won't hesitate to share the world
My dream–you are the one that came true.

Stars at night, shimmering high,
Mirroring love in the midnight sky.
Under the moon, where kisses fall,
Your smile, my heaven…my all.

Midnight whiskey blues.

Is it true, my love, what they say?
That you've lost your faith in me?
I will play the violin for you,
When you're going to run to another man…

Since you left me in the darkness, baby!
I've been drowning myself in whiskey blues…
Never to expect anything anymore, I lie to myself,
Just so that I can hurt you more.

Goodbye, my sunshine,
Farewell to dreams that won't come true.
I close my eyes, too weary to watch,
Just to not see you walk away from me again.

Alone and guilty, lost in my sins,
Letting whiskey speak my truth.
They see a man standing tall,
But inside, I'm just a beggar for salvation.

A sorrowful beauty, yet somehow healing,
That restless fire burning deep.
Etched in the walls, our fading love,
Yet it's all good when the midnight whiskey blues echoes.

A perfect day.

Lost but found, turned around,
Falling fast without a sound.
Shaken, twisted, yet I stand,
Fucked, but I feel so grand.

As long as my glass stays full,
My heart stays cold; my mind is dull.
This isn't a habit, isn't a sin,
You're the problem, not the gin.

Two decades in, we still ride,
From classroom days to streets outside…
We live it up, no time to borrow,
Jesus didn't turn water to milk.

One, then two, then three, then more,
No need to rush, just let it pour.
The gods have blessed me with their wine,
And now it's theirs as much as mine.

A drink made me, so I think.
She holds me close; she lets me sink.
Me and my bottle, we're okay.
Just another perfect day.

A timeless bloom.

Beneath the sky where starlight gleams,
Breathes a heart wrapped in dreams…
A soul so benign as the breeze,
Her laughter dances through the echoes of the trees.

Her eyes, like twilights gentle embrace,
Hold within a peaceful grace…
Her kindness spreads a soft refrain,
Like tender drops of summer rain.

As flowers bloom the earth she walks through.
Morning skies filled with golden hues,
Where nectar is plenty and love stretched each mile,
Through every storm, through every fight.

Her voice, a song of whispered stream's,
Rippling through the silence of love,
Birth's a joy so light, so rare…
In every tear, in every smile.

In the quiet moments, you linger near,
A presence felt though you are not here…
Like a warmth that swathes the night,
To a timeless bloom, I surrender myself.

Alchemy of a broken girl.

Like a phoenix, her wings ablaze,
A burden of fire she wears with grace.
Among a thousand watching shadows,
She burns bright, defiant, like an eclipse.

A past that lingers, haunts her still,
But one sacred cry keeps her soul intact.
She whispers prayers to skies above,
Finds peace in arms that hold her back.

To forget, she paints a smile,
In neon lights, in fleeting nights,
In touches, tastes, and pulsing sound,
She dances till she's heaven-bound.

Fear and doubt, they claw inside,
Toxic thoughts she learns to fight.
Still, in her fury, she found release,
Her wrath became her path to peace.

Heart once shattered, never again,
The lessons carved in silent pain.
Called a fool, but hope remains,
To trust, to feel, to love unchained.

Her strength, a flame that lights the dark,
Her path is forged with fire and heart.
She rises not just to survive,
But to be loved,
And love,
Alive.

The shape of forever.

She wears the sunshine on her face,
Her sweet heart radiates the beautiful escape...
With every smile, the world feels right,
She is my dawn, my guiding light.

Is she the one to whom I surrender?
A love too true to comprehend.
Without her breath, I cease to be…
She is the pulse that steadies me.

When I met her, it's was lust,
A day forward more, it's only her I yearn…
I gave my all, she made me whole,
My warmth, my dream, my love forever be.

A decade danced in love's embrace,
Still, each glance quickens my pace.
Butterflies stir as twilight nears,
Sunsets kiss our golden years.

Eternal bliss, my forever bride…
My wife, the eyes of my unborn child,
Forevermore, I'm yours to stay,
As everglades embrace the day.

Ashes of the honest.

Are you not ashamed, my love?
Or did I steal your shyness, sip by sip!
Left you stained, soul-deep and shimmering,
With all our perfect flaws.
Touch your heart and tell me the truth…
Did we ever burn for nothing?

Every step I walk brings me closer to what I am running from.
Like it's dragging me back to my shackles once again…
Rust-bitten roads spitting fire and dust in
redemption's name…
Nowhere found on any map I trust.

A man unmade by the love that should support?
Instead unstitched me, thread by thread.
Buried underneath the moulding sins,
The edge is the only place I find home.

A prayer to lie to myself, I blabber.
Is it a comfort or a gesture of some pantaloons?
It doesn't matter, I won't pretend…
So long as you recall the cost of staying sane.

When the silence roars, the hymn echoes…

A repeated word, a world in chasm.

Still to whom is the hell bound?

To a goddess who closed her eyes, worshipping shadows mistaken for light.

Diamonds at dusk.

Nobody can make her stay,
She belongs to no one.
She leaves you breathless…
All she wants is the money by the morning light.

Next time you glimpse her,
A run free from moonshine...
She swallows like a good girl,
Never to spill the beans on you.

Or am I the one lost, seeking softer fires?
She stands, rooted like stone,
Nothing ever flames her ego…
A good girl in a hell's sake bound.

She let her shyness go when the dusk hits,
Emotions entangle when passion flees…
Her nudeness in gold,
All she wants is to shine like a diamond.

Through doors uncounted, she walks one dream,
Frozen heart but the hands stay warm for each touch,
For only wealth, she's come to trust,
A diamond's shine in paper dust.

Driftwood dreams.

The wind has snuffed the candle's flame,
The light within me fades to shame.
Behind this bottle of liquid grace,
I hide my truth; I mask my face.

Just to numb my feelings.

Like driftwood caught in an icy stream,
Hollow within, devoid of dreams.
Yet in the stillness, numbness grew,
A transient comfort where cold winds blew.

Just to numb my feelings.

Above the haze, beyond distant cries,
Shadows twist as smoke takes to the skies.
A spark of worth roars through the night,
Piercing clouds of doubt with fleeting light.

Just to numb my feelings.

Is this what it means to belong?
Hands entwined, yet the rhythm feels wrong.
A puzzle unsolved, what do I seek?

Lost between the real and the solace I keep.

Just to numb my feelings.

The world's echoes paint my mind,
A spark of joy, so rare to find.
Tears fall like sunshine, a warm release.
Is this love real, or a vision insincere?

Just to numb my feelings.

Drunk on desire.

Take me by my broken heart,
Wash me clean off my sin...
Sex me till I shut my eyes,
Lie to me, you love me till I am sober.

Velvet drapes and tongues of gold,
Smoke and spirits, stories told.
Barefoot on the city stone,
A heart that dreams but walks alone.

Like a beacon of light in the deepest of seas.
Shining as bright as the moon on the seas.
Golden like sunlight that ripples on streams,
You are a rush that flows in my veins.

Her love, a fire wild and free,
Pulls me under, endlessly.
A spark, a storm, a fleeting bliss,
Lost within her deadly kiss.

Every touch, every trace,
Wrapped in the warmth of her embrace.
Kiss me softly, slow and deep,
Until I drift away in sleep.

Love me like a lie.

Found her among the flock,
A perfect stranger to a mistress…
The breeze adores her flowing trail,
A river of beauty, pure and pale.

Moonlight wove through golden strands,
Soft as whispers, light as sand.
Between the dusk and breaking dawn,
Her nudeness sings, beyond comparison.

No crown she needs, no diamonds rare,
Is this fate or a glimpse of passion?
Sex never tasted sweet,
Her naked soul, a sacred crime.

She gave me companionship when my heart longed lust,
Stoned enough to see things in rose tinted glasses,
A flower waiting to be plucked again and again…
Rooted in sin that bloomed to a beautiful wildflower.

I stole her breath, led her astray,
Where shadows dance and angel's fray.
Bare and free, she fell to me,
Crying, "Love me, break me, set me free."

Confined desires.

I grew up around sinners,
In a house never called home…
Weighted thoughts suffocated hope,
While shattered dreams drowned at the bottom of a bottle.

The falling never stops…
In this pitfall, the needle rips a hole!
Hate clouding my eyes,
I lie awake but there is no one to sing a lullaby.

Where shadows swayed and whispers hung in the air,
Happiness and laughter banished altogether.
Leaving behind just silence,
To benumbed without remorse.

The monster under my bed is still blemished,
No one seems to comprehend!
Now all I pray is someone to hold me,
As I am drifting away from my own reality.

A threat that worsens under pressure,
A danger that deepens with stress…
To find love within is the only answer,
For I yearn to escape from these confines.

Echoes of a withered soul.

The abyss that I am in got me spending,
Falling deep with no forewarning,
Overdosing in emotions raw,
Numbing pain I can't ignore.

I took her path to sin!
Dressed it up, yet felt the same,
Trapped within this reckless mess,
Still, I chase it nonetheless.

The sun has rose,
Another dawn of silence took its toll,
No words are left to bridge the space,
Only the rhythm of our bodies talks.

Different faces, different eyes,
Different hearts with different cries,
Yet I love them all alike,
Only to deny the ties.

I will let you go in time,
Find our hearts depart divine...
In this withered madness, I feel alive.
Is this what I have become?

Stay with me.

Here I wait, still and longing,
For a voice that once set me singing…
A lullaby beneath the fire's glow,
Burning with a love only we know.

You are the one, the spark in my night,
The colours that filled my world with light.
You make my heart lose its steady beat,
And every day, I pray our souls will meet.

I want you near, close enough to feel,
To melt into love that's raw and real.
For it is only you, my heart's true choice,
The one who drowns my fears with a voice.

You saw my scars, yet still you stayed,
And I'll take you whole, unafraid.
Let's surrender to the hush of the night,
Where our bodies sing in soft moonlight.

From the first kiss to this very breath,
You hold my soul; don't let it rest.
For life without you would fade away,
So let me be the reason you stay.

Ephemeral desire.

I found her on a silent night,
A spark that set the stars alight…
Bodies swayed in whispered fire,
Moved by rhythm, touched by desire.

Two souls apart, yet fate entwined,
A moment brief, yet so divine.
A single touch, a fleeting taste,
Left me lost in passion's embrace.

She held me close through endless gloom,
A beacon bright in tangled doom.
Her warmth, the solace I would seek.
A memory mine alone to keep.

Her scent, like roses, rich and sweet,
Her touch, a fire, wild and complete.
Her breath tales' new horizons,
The heat between her thighs makes me vulnerable.

Is she the one? I do not know,
For love like hers is meant to flow.
She is the dream that fades with dawn,
A love to cherish, yet never own.

Echoes of you.

In her, my heart finds solace sweet,
A soul so pure, no shadows meet!
With you, I find myself bewitched in…
You are a reflection of beauty in every sense.

This is not the first time I've felt...
But I hope the last, my rhythm beats!
In her presence, love's eternal gleam,
Her touch, a calm whispering stream.

A smile that dances like the morning light,
Eyes that sparkle like stars of the night,
Lips of roses, soft and red…
Graceful as the cupid's humble kiss.

With every step, a melody,
Her breath, a symphony…
With each glance, hearts flutter,
Making us enrapture.

The warmth of her spirit mushrooming like the sun's honeyed kiss…
A haven of bliss in her embrace!
Nurturing the soul's cape,
Of one's drifting in the echoes of you.

Etched in the haze.

I am but a man of tears,
A shallow stream strewn with jagged rocks...
Will there be respite in this fiery storm?
For my weary legs ache without a halt.

The writing on the walls stifles the breath,
A haze of thoughts distorts what's real.
A thrill long lost,
A dream that clings, unsure, unbelieving.

Now I am free to sin,
A freedom born of my own design.
Regret lingers like a shadow of life-
Or is forgiveness the lie we chase in the light?

Withered mind subdued to reality,
A place unknown to heart.
Foolish, yet far from wrong...
What once loved is never gone.

Echoes of unity amidst turbulent thoughts,
As time, fear keeps conjuring the old…
A time to release and a time to hold fast!
Of what's etched in stone.

Endless reverie.

I have nothing left to say,
No words left for my heart to break…
Nor do I have any more sensation!
No stones unturned, still I feel befuddled.

As night falls, I feel temptations rising…
A silent storm within the air.
Forgetting my pain, I sin again…
Your neck on my lips, a reckless prayer.

Sweet bites but this isn't love!
Just a man on lesser grounds…
The quiet stretches through the night,
Just numbing to be someone else in your eyes.

Where nothing is as I breathe to see,
Passing through days by the bottle that I abuse,
To hear her cry, to feel her warmth…
To fill the void of the emptiness I am.

Reminiscing to dream the same dream again,
Just to feel the shared feelings we once shared enthusiastically…
For me to close my eyes peacefully,
Alone, in endless reverie.

Sinnerman's paradise.

She is the one I long to be within,
Drowned in her love, her fire, her sin.
Her first kiss, her lingering touch,
Her eyes-so deep, they steal my breath.

Lost within the warmth of her lips,
A thousand blossoms bloom and drip.
Naked and unchained, pure and free,
My heart, I offer, willingly.

No rush of a needle, no fleeting high,
Could match the spark when she draws nigh.
Her touch, the gravity that keeps me bound,
Her breath, the flame that lifts me higher.

In her tongue I was lost…
The nectar of a thousand flowers blossomed…
Bare and free, pure and unconditional,
My heart, I lay down.

Into her lust, I slip and sway,
Where golden dreams in shadows play.
I lay beside her, lost in time,
In sinnerman's paradise, divine.

Horizon of lust.

She shivers beneath my touch,
Dripping like a summer storm,
A rainbow arching over my head,
Her light seeped into my shadowed heart.

Our minds race past the horizon,
She craves me, unchained, untamed–boom.
Like roses in bloom on Valentine's night,
She strips the thorns from my frozen soul.

Shades of lust winds the air,
Where longing bends to pleasure.
Like ice succumbing to fire,
She melts me into something new.

Is it guilt? Is it sin?
Wisdom, or just the fear of surrender?
But the sway of her hips is a spell,
and I am caught, helpless.

Lips locked in the nectar of her,
For in her, the warmth feels different…
One touch, and I'm spiralling,
With her, I find completion…and my release.

Love lit at first kiss.

Each morning, I greet the world with love,
Waking with a smirk, the sky singing bright blue.
Grateful breaths in morning's grace,
Humbled by nature's evergreen embrace.

She found me when our youth was new,
In golden hours, our spirits flew.
Our first kiss, lit flames inside,
Since then, with Mary, I've always abided.

We danced through dreams, clouds beneath,
Laughed aloud with Ganja for breath.
Eyes aglow, the smoke would swirl,
A rebel in a spinning world.

Together we soared with sun and the moon,
In her rhythm, I belong.
That 4/20 we grooved on cloud nine,
The world stood still, her soul in mine.

With Mary, it's love that never tires,
A bond that burns with endless blaze.
Through every breath and every part,
It's her and I, till death do us part.

City of ghosts.

Deserted in the big city…
Lost in the traffic of our soul,
Too many signals trying to stop,
When I am just fading away with the light.

I am so lonely in this house that's never a home,
Four walls and ceilings are closing in on me,
Whispering to open the door,
To see a rainbow beyond my perception.

A leap of faith to push past my own limits,
I keep trying but nothing seems to be conjured.
Feels like I am been pulled apart from the inside,
Yet I remain unbiased, cooped away from the world.

Is it fear that I stopped or am I just outgrown to feel shy,
A remorseless life I tasted was sweet,
But in the end, it is I who rots.

A thousand beds with different views,
All felt the same except my bleeding heart…
But when the moonlight shines its rays,
I am awake again.

Mama bird.

You are the desert rose that bloomed my soul,
Holding me close, yet keeping me still.
A dewdrop to quench my thirst,
Yet our eyes never truly met.

The distance feels so nearby…
You and I, two peas in a pod,
Yet love tastes so bittersweet,
Lingering on my tongue like a memory.

You are the only one I confide in,
My darkness, yet my freedom.
From the moment I saw you beneath the church bells,
Two decades later, my heart still beats reckless.

A stranger became a friend,
A friend became a secret love.
Through nights of silent despair,
I wrestled with the thought of losing you.

Now, as time drifts like a cold breeze,
My heart feels blistered without your warmth.
Yet, you never let go,
You hold me close, like a mama bird to her own.

Heroin.

I have been abandoned, I have seen…
A home, shattered with guilt.
Lost in the crossroads between,
A life built without trust.

Seasons shift like fleeting emotions,
A fickle past undone…
But is that what I am?
When pain conjures reality!

A faded page, blank yet stained,
Forgotten, though echoes remain.
A needle shatters fragile peace,
Between love and hate, joy and pain.

Shadows of sorrow take their hold,
Fearing the darkness yet untold…
Family ties and bonds!!
The only remains less of a suicidal thought.

Now I breathe, fresh and unbiased…
Yet, love brings fire…
A cleanse from my desires…
To love and be loved, my heart aspires.

Tempest within.

Raised on the wrong side of the bed...
Each dawn begins with a shadowed mood,
A fog so thick, I fail to see the good.
My anger tears through tranquil skies,
A tempest raging where calmness lies.

Trapped within the confines of cliché,
A phase that never fades with the day.
Still rising to face this fractured scene,
A dreamer lost in what might have been.

Branded desperate, labelled insane,
Too weary to counter their disdain.
Is this humility's final test?
Or apathy's hand clutching my chest?

Entangled in a world astray,
Where the twisted thrive, and the good decay.
A flicker of joy in the shadowed abyss,
Bound by rules we hardly miss.

When hatred roots too deep to tame,
No balm exists to soothe the flame.
Perhaps salvation lies ahead,
In waking up on the other side of the bed.

Let it be.

I am empty today, like a hollow palm,
Drained of echoes, nothing to mend.
Yet the thought of you, my love,
Keeps the fire within from fading.

Storms rage, chaos lingers,
Pulling me deeper into the void.
Like a jester lost in madness,
I chase illusions to feel alive.

But since you stepped into my world,
Strangeness feels a little less cruel.
Words are wisdom, it's imperative…
Yet, I am lost at the sight of you.

Between the cries, I hear you…
Showing me the meaning of being together,
Your voice, a wildflower bloomed...
Showering me with unbiased love.

In this calm rage, a beautiful story remains,
A whispered tale among the stars.
Without you, the world seems distant,
So come take my hand and let it be.

Infinite longing.

Each day begins with thoughts of you,
A love so pure, alive, and true.
The shadows I wore are now laid to rest,
For in your light, my soul's ablaze.

I yearn for your touch, your warm embrace,
Though echoes may part, we share this space.
Our hearts entwined, a love divine,
I am forever yours and you forever loved.

When trust isn't won with words alone,
But my heart beats with love unbroken.
No words can change what's come and gone,
But my shadows fade with each new dawn.

I've never known peace like the nights we shared,
When dreams feel real, and nothing compares.
You complete me in ways I can't explain,
A kiss for my soul, soothing the pain.

When the sun hugs the sky and the moon smiles,
I long for the sound of your heartbeat.
Like a shooting star with a hope,
I want to close my eyes with you beside.

The echoing whispers.

Blazing fiercely till shadows fade away,
Clinging to hope without regret or sway...
Unyielding and proud as the world bends low,
A wicked dawn greets with a sinister glow.

Drifting through the silent nights,
Whispering why it's not alright.
Risking all for a fleeting touch,
Fading dreams in softened light.

Chasing more with blinded sight,
Hoping too much as the world flies by,
Bruised by the weight of rejection's bite,
Yet never too proud to give it one more tries.

A fathomless chasm, vast and deep,
Where whispers of thought gently creep...
These hands have felt the warmth of skin,
Yet my heart has never touched within.

Now I feel nothing but the emptiness,
A shallow blind river where I wet my feet,
Thinking time will wash away my sin.
A freedom from this empty vessel I dream.

What love still knows.

And so, he stood, waiting,
One last glance, one last chance-
This time, he swore,
He wouldn't break what was already shattered.

Two hearts, one soul, now frayed,
Her breath once quieted his storms.
She held his hand, when the silence screamed too loud,
When the echoes of his past grew loud.

Yet for all her light, he was a shadow,
Drowning in bottles, numbed by dust.
She reached, she fought,
But he was too blind to see.

Seasons turned, moons faded,
Hearts once loved, still beats...
One touch, and the darkness faltered-
The wicked found his way home.

Now he stands, stripped of pride and broken,
She lingers, fearing old ghosts.
But he waits, he prays,
For she is the grace in his madness.

The numb king.

I am the dog, God created to bark,
I buck back, don't rile me up!
I chase the dusk till the moon weeps…
I ball the court whole royally.

Is it the past, or my shadow staring back?
Pills dull the weight of being,
Where memory fades like whispers in smoke,
And overdose feels like a lover's touch.

Lost in the maze of my own mind!
I fumble and rumble, making a ripple.
Building and breaking in the same breath,
Just to wake up to an unknown reality.

Different temperatures, different tastes!
Her scent of sin lingers, my senses…
The warmth of her lust keeps me sane…
Hit it back and forth like Mary jane.

If no door opens, I tear through the walls,
No stones unturned, only echoes and sparks.
Silver and gold drape my bones,
But all this fire is turning me numb.

My Insanity.

The morning spins, surreal and thin,
As if I'm floating deep within.
I slit the silence, chasing peace-
But find no end, no sweet release.

Thoughts spiral, dark and undefined,
Is it madness, or a fractured mind?
Addict or ghost, I cannot tell,
I beg for love to break the spell.

We scream for change, but stay the same,
Two halves lost in a broken name.
Torn between the truth and lies,
Haunted by yesterday's disguise.

Something crawls beneath my flesh,
A creeping itch I can't suppress.
My skin turns pale, my heart feels dead,
Reflections scream the words unsaid.

Dreams and waking start to blend,
As sanity begins to bend.
I speak to shadows by my bed,
They laugh, then whisper in my head.

"Let go," I cry, "let me be free–
Or leave me lost in my insanity.

Growing old with you.

On a Sunday, I woke to love's embrace,
A warmth that filled me, a sacred space,
A feeling so deep, beyond my reach,
Like tasting the salt of earth's soft speech.
Mondays now hold a different light,
Like I've been given a double shot of delight,
A simple smile, a joyful spark,
With her, this world feels safe and stark.
In her eyes, I see our future unfold,
Without words, it feels so bold,
A Tuesday turned to magic in her arms,
A beautiful tomorrow, untouched by harm.
Wednesday brought the sun's pure glow,
Birds in chorus, and butterflies flow,
On my knees, I held her hand tight,
Pouring my heart, under love's light.
On a Thursday, in summer's sweet embrace,
I gave her my hope, and found my place,
Love never tasted so pure, so right,
Until she stole my heart that night.
The weekend came with familiar cheer,
Friends and family, took the Friday row,
One day I'll have to let her go,
But until then, my love will only grow.

With her, I feel like a Saturday night,
A sunrise tequila, burning bright at dawns break!
Day by day, I am getting more normal with you...
Guess that's the best feeling growing old with you.

No map for the lost.

In a world untamed,
I chase the wind through dreamscapes free,
No limits to a thousand thoughts,
Where I make up stories in my head to escape reality.

Sometimes I feel like a one-way street,
No stars above to see the path ahead,
Loneliness lingers in quiet echoes,
Draped in shades of endless night.

The coldness of the hearts unchained,
Chills the summer breeze…
Awake and awkward, moments fleet…
Unbiased with the different kisses.

Material drugs don't shut the voices anymore!
No borrowed scents can bring me home,
Is it that hard to love again?
Or in your arms, have I outgrown my own?

Yet through the haze, I find my calm,
A fragile thread of truth unseen of who we are deep inside!
Like mirrors catching fading light,
A wait with endless wishes.

Ten toes on fate.

Fear weighed heavy as I drowned in sorrow,
Refusing to set me free…
Clinging like a shadow at dusk,
My own reflection haunts, my past still speaks in echoes.

Taunting of the past traumatize,
Still turning the page around,
Living everyday like the bloom of a new bud!
For the moment I made peace with my sins, I was born again.

Where and when, yet why lingers on,
Waking at dawn with ghosts of the lost.
If I lose myself again,
Would you hold me close till the silence returns?

Sands under my feet still holds me,
Ten toes on fate.
Mind maybe lucid but hearts don't panic,
Where knees don't bend and heads don't bow.

Now my thought is clear but the sight of the destination is still blur,
Where should I go from here?
To make love or to make war!
When all I truly want is to wake up next to you.

The bittersweet tale of us.

Fairy tale beginnings, both sweet and fleeting,
A first smile blossoming into soft kisses...
From shivers down spines to sorrows unyielding,
Yet shaping us whole in the journey's embraces.

Roses bloomed, their thorns entwining,
Life once dull, untouched by hues…
Until you cast rainbows upon my horizon,
Beauty seen through love's softened view.

Like dewdrops quenching morning glories,
Your nectar stirred my restless soul…
A hummingbird thirsting for more,
Ready to fall to Cupid's cruel bow.

Our names were once a tranquil story,
Yet mistakes led us down narrow roads…
Blinded by desire, lost in longing,
Parched without your golden glow.

What goes around must come again,
Past sins paving the path for anew…
But as sadness fades grey the moment you return,
I tell myself this, to veil my heart's truth...

Where promises drift.

Time unravels when love is torn,
Memories hum, tattered and worn.
With you, I tasted what love could mean,
Yet still, I chase a distant dream.

One more horizon's hue kissed by the dawn.
Another bottle cracked with harmonious sound,
A rockstar's dream, alive and loud,
But without you, the music is lost in the crowd.

Your scent still lingers on my bed,
Echoes of all the words we said.
I live for vows we swore to keep…
Though love may break, it does not sleep.

Where right turned wrong and gold to grey,
Our promises were swept away.
Alone, despair carved deep and wide,
But faith still flickers in your eyes.

Knee-deep in sin, I lose the fight,
Your touch still pulls me back to light.
You catch me even as I stray,
Though like tides, I wash away.

We drowned in tears we could not name,
Still yearning to be cleansed by rain.
Is it whiskey's warmth or her soft face
That mourns me in my hollow place?

When night arrives and dreams have wept,
The silence is all that's truly kept.

The hollow puzzle.

I've shackled myself in this infernal mire.
Drowning my soul in ceaseless fire.
Flickering thoughts of the past still bloom in darkness…
In this madness I remain.

Pills and dust ease the existence…
Reality fades, a broken trust.
Bodies change, yet hearts don't meet,
Mine beats hollow, unbleached.

What once felt love, now hate trembles.
A thought to love again, haunts!
The puzzle is still unfinished,
The hole never fit the missing piece.

Deep in vain, in crimson wine I sink!
Dine with another man's wife…
Where insanity is my sane…
In sin, I find my madness the same.

Like a feather in this withered storm,
Unable to rise burdened down with self-pity.
I find solace in oneself in the truth I believe!
That, you are never alone when shadows breathe.

Where the wind breaks.

Where I dwell is home enough,
A thousand beds with tales of gold…
A different view from every window,
All the same as long as I let go.

All these years I've felt it most,
A story that goes on etched in the walls…
Never to break, never to spill,
I vowed to sink with what befalls.

Lately I have been doing better,
A warmth within the winter's air,
A shiver dances down my spine,
And on my lips, a quiet grin.

The tunnel's end is clear and bright,
No shadow masks the open way.
One step could free me from the past…
But then I realise, I am not chained.

So, what is it I truly fear?
A simple life or not living while I am alive?
Like a petal borne upon the breeze,
I am drifting to where the wind breaks.

Woven in Time.

Another day fades by without you near,
Yearning for your touch, your voice so dear.
Her laughter, soft as a morning's light,
Turns even the darkest moments bright.

To bare my soul, no walls remain,
Lost in your gaze, where hearts unchain.
More than a wish, more than a dream,
You and I, love's endless stream.

The seasons change, carried by the wind's kiss.
Moons rise high! Is there hope for me?
The stars above in silence shine,
While butterflies dance and bees align.

Thoughts of despair disappear with you here,
Desire transcends in a warm embrace.
Where emotions entangle passions fire,
I see my head laid in your laps.

It's hard to fall in love again,
Yet trust and faith still linger inside.
It's you I long for, now and always,
For in your arms, my heart resides.

The echoing now.

I can't let go of who I've become,
But I can rest my burdens down…
The sins I blew smoke in younger days,
Shaped this soul that stands here now.

The present is all that truly matters,
The past, a storm we cannot calm.
We drown in echoes, dry of tears,
But why,
When hope still blooms in the now?

I push forward, breathless with purpose, rooted to what I stand but I am not grounded,
Freedom isn't an illusion to the one who belongs,
Who's found their place, their voice, their time.

Young and dumb I rode with all my peers,
Smoke to ashes, no more higher level from this,
Pleasure so euphoric, lust so blissed.
But this is me now, I burn far brighter.

So, for the journey ahead, I rise renewed,
With calm resolve, I chase what's true.
I see the love, vivid and alive,
And feel my echoing reflection whole now, unflawed.

Lost dogs go to heaven.

Am I the broken or the blessed?
A victor crowned, or just obsessed,
With dreams too vivid to be real,
This world revolts, and none can heal.

In dawn's pale hush I stand alone,
Regret a weight I've come to own.
My heartbeat stumbles in the silence,
Longing for a softer brush.

Between the thorns where roses grow,
I bleed the love you'll never know.
Something inside begins to tear,
Fading slow with every stare.

In emptiness, I make my bed,
My only lover, madness fed.
No more wishes, no more flame,
Each day returns, numb and the same.

But still, the stars in silence gleam,
Whispering life into the dream.
A flicker stirs beyond the strife,
A hint of grace, a taste of life.

Maybe the lost aren't truly gone,
Maybe we will find heaven all along.